A Christmas Manger

by H. A. Rey

With Text from Matthew and Luke

A New Kind of Punch-Out-and-Play Book

NOTHING TO PASTE—JUST FOLD!

HOUGHTON MIFFLIN BOOKS FOR CHILDREN

Houghton Mifflin Harcourt

BOSTON | NEW YORK

nd it came to pass in those days, that there went out a decree from Caesar Augustus, that all the world should be taxed. And all went to be taxed, every one into his own city. And Joseph also went up from Galilee, out of the city of Nazareth, into Judaea, unto the city of David, which is called Bethlehem, to be taxed, with Mary his wife.

And she brought forth her firstborn son, and wrapped him in swaddling clothes, and laid him in a manger; because there was no room for them in the inn.

Now when Jesus was born in Bethlehem of Judaea in the days of Herod the king, behold, there came wise men from the east to Jerusalem, saying, "Where is he that is born King of the Jews? for we have seen his star in the east and are come to worship him."

They departed, and, lo, the star, which they saw in the east, went before them, till it came and stood over where the young child was. When they saw the star they rejoiced with exceeding great joy.

And they saw the young child with Mary his mother, and fell down, and worshipped him: and when they had opened their treasures, they presented unto him gifts; gold, and frankincense, and myrrh.

And there were in the same country shepherds abiding in the field, keeping watch over their flock by night. And, lo, the angel of the Lord came upon them, and the glory of the Lord shone round about them: and they were sore afraid. And the angel said unto them, "Fear not: for, behold, I bring you good tidings of great joy, which shall be to all people. For unto you is born this day in the city of David a Saviour, which is Christ the Lord. And this shall be a sign unto you; Ye shall find the babe wrapped in swaddling clothes, lying in a manger."

And suddenly there was with the angel a multitude of the heavenly host praising God, and saying, "Glory to God in the highest, and on earth peace to men of good will."

And it came to pass, as the angels were gone away from them into heaven, the shepherds said one to another, "Let us now go even unto Bethlehem, and see this thing which is come to pass, which the Lord hath made known unto us." And they came with haste and found Mary, and Joseph, and the babe lying in a manger.

And when they had seen it they made known abroad the saying which was told them concerning this child. And all they that heard it wondered at those things which were told them by the shepherds. But Mary kept all these things, and pondered them in her heart.

And the shepherds returned, glorifying and praising God for all the things that they had heard and seen, as it was told unto them.

From Matthew 2 and Luke 2.

fold up

fold up

put ends through slits

like this: